A Note to Parents

Your child is beginning the lifelong adventure of reading! And with the **World of Reading** program, you can be sure that he or she is receiving the encouragement needed to become a confident, independent reader. This program is specially designed to encourage your child to enjoy reading at every level by combining exciting, easy-to-read stories featuring favorite characters with colorful art that brings the magic to life.

The **World of Reading** program is divided into four levels so that children at any stage can enjoy a successful reading experience:

Reader-in-Training
Pre-K–Kindergarten
Picture reading and word repetition for children who are getting ready to read.

Beginner Reader
Pre-K–Grade 1
Simple stories and easy-to-sound-out words for children who are just learning to read.

Junior Reader
Kindergarten–Grade 2
Slightly longer stories and more varied sentences perfect for children who are reading with the help of a parent.

Super Reader
Grade 1–Grade 3
Encourages independent reading with rich story lines and wide vocabulary that's right for children who are reading on their own.

Learning to read is a once-in-a-lifetime adventure, and with **World of Reading**, the journey is just beginning!

Copyright © 2013 Disney Enterprises, Inc.
All rights reserved. Published by Disney Press, an imprint of Disney Book Group. No part of this book may
be reproduced or transmitted in any form or by any means, electronic or mechanical, including photocopying,
recording, or by any information storage and retrieval system, without written permission from the publisher.
For information address Disney Press, 1101 Flower Street, Glendale, California 91201.
Printed in the United States of America
First Edition
1 3 5 7 9 10 8 6 4 2
G658-7729-4-13227
Library of Congress Catalog Card Number: 2012937002
ISBN 978-1-4231-6964-2

For more Disney Press fun, visit www.disneybooks.com

SUSTAINABLE
FORESTRY
INITIATIVE
Certified Chain of Custody
Promoting Sustainable Forestry
www.sfiprogram.org
SFI-01415
The SFI label applies to the text stock

World of Reading

LEVEL 2

DISNEP
MICKEY & FRIENDS

Goofy's
Sledding Contest

By Kate Ritchey
Illustrated by Loter Inc.
and the Disney Storybook Artists

DISNEP PRESS
New York • Los Angeles

One chilly morning,
Goofy woke up to find
snow outside his window.

"Yahoo!" he yelled
    as he jumped out of bed.
"Winter is here!"

Goofy loved the winter.
He loved getting bundled up
in his warmest clothes.

He loved building snowmen
and the crunch the snow made
as he walked through it.

But Goofy's favorite thing
was sledding!

Goofy looked at his sleds.
They were all fun to ride,
but he wondered if there was
a faster way down the hill.

Goofy dug through his closet,
looking for something that
would be slippery enough.
He found just the thing. . . .

His surfboard!

Goofy ran outside and up a hill.

He put the surfboard on the ground,

jumped up on it, and . . .

. . . sank!
The surfboard was too heavy!
"Gosh," said Goofy.
"I guess I need to find
something different."

Goofy thought and thought.
Then he had an idea.
Goofy got two bananas.
He put the peels on his feet
and took a step forward.

Bam! Goofy slipped on the peels
and fell backward into the snow.
"Ouch!" he said.
"I guess I slip on banana peels,
but they do not slip on snow."

Just then, Mickey came along.
"Why are you lying in the snow?"
he asked Goofy.

"I was trying to find
the fastest way down the hill,"
Goofy explained.

"Hmmm," Mickey said.
"I have a racing sled
that is very fast.
You could try that."

"Thank you, Mickey," said Goofy.
"I wonder if it is faster
than my sleds.
We should have a race!"

Goofy decided to invite
all his friends to race.
Goofy called Minnie.
Then Minnie called Daisy.
And Daisy called Donald.
Everyone was excited!

Goofy's friends looked for
things to race on.
Mickey took out his sled.

Donald found a blow-up raft.

Minnie and Daisy chose
a sled with two seats.

Goofy tried and tried to find
something faster than a sled.
But nothing worked.
Maybe a sled was best,
after all.

But which of his sleds
should Goofy bring with him?
A saucer? A toboggan?
A tube?

Goofy could not decide.
So he piled his sleds
into a laundry basket
and dragged them all to the park.

When Goofy arrived,
Minnie and Daisy were
making a snowman.
"He can judge the race,"
said Minnie.

Mickey and Donald were having
a snowball fight.
"Hi, Goofy! Ready to race?"
asked Donald, peeking out
from behind a tree. Smack!
He was hit by Mickey's snowball!

At the top of the hill,
the friends got ready to race.
Goofy took his sleds
out of the basket.
It was time to pick one!

"Everybody ready?" Mickey said.
"On your marks,
get set . . ."
But Goofy was not ready!
He turned to Mickey
to ask him to wait . . .

. . . and fell right into
his laundry basket.
"GO!" yelled Mickey.
"Whoops!" yelled Goofy.
The race had started without him!

Just then, the basket
started slipping down the hill.
It moved faster and faster.
Goofy slid past his friends.

Goofy looked around.
He was in the lead!
His ears blew back in the wind.
Snow flew up all around him.

"Yahoo!" he yelled.
He raced past the snowman
at the bottom of the hill.
Goofy had won!

"You were so fast!" Mickey said.
"How did you think of using
a laundry basket?" asked Minnie.
Goofy smiled. "I guess you could say
I just stumbled into it!"